This book belongs to

. . . .

Illustrations by Priscilla Lamont

Every effort has been made to trace the ownership of all material. In the event
of any question arising as to the use of the material, the publisher will be happy to make the
necessary correction for use in future printings.

This edition published by Parragon in 2010
Parragon
Queen Street House
4 Queen Street
Bath BA1 1HE, UK

Copyright © Parragon Books Ltd 2008

ISBN 978-1-4454-0895-8
Printed in China

MOTHER GOOSE TREASURY

Bath New York Singapore Hong Kong Cologne Delhi Melbourne

Mother Goose

For centuries Mother Goose has been gathering a collection of magical, well-loved tales. Journey to remarkable places and faraway lands with her to meet all kinds of wonderful people and animals, and see the words come to life.

Parents and grandparents can relive their special childhood moments by reading and sharing these classic nursery rhymes with their children and grandchildren. People can always remember a nursery rhyme. These wonderful rhymes will stay with you forever.

Contents

Old Mother Goose

Old Mother Goose,
When she wanted to wander,
Would ride through the air
On a very fine gander.

Mother Goose had a house,
It stood in the wood,
Where an owl at the door
As a sentinel stood.

She had a son, Jack,
A plain looking lad.
He was not very good,
Nor yet very bad.

She sent him to market,
A live goose he bought.
"See, Mother," he said,
"I have not been for naught."

Jack's goose and her gander,
Soon grew very fond.
They'd both eat together,
Or swim in the pond.

Then, one fine morning,
As I have been told,
Jack's goose had laid him
An egg of pure gold.

Little Bo-Peep

Little Bo-Peep has lost her sheep,

And doesn't know where to find them;

Leave them alone,

And they'll come home,

Wagging their tails behind them.

Little Boy Blue

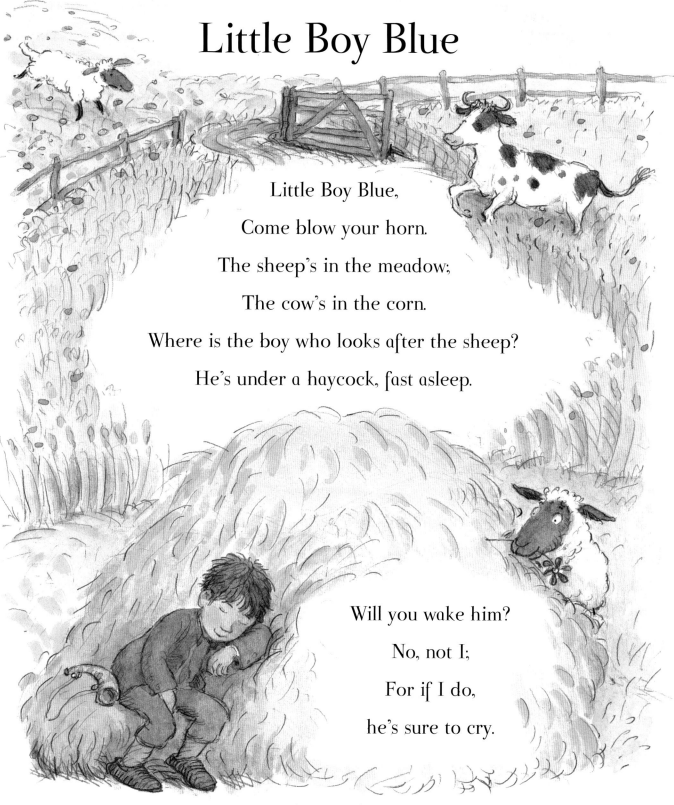

Little Boy Blue,

Come blow your horn.

The sheep's in the meadow;

The cow's in the corn.

Where is the boy who looks after the sheep?

He's under a haycock, fast asleep.

Will you wake him?

No, not I;

For if I do,

he's sure to cry.

A-Tisket A-Tasket

A-tisket a-tasket,

A green and yellow basket.

I wrote a letter to my love,

And on the way I dropped it.

I dropped it, I dropped it,

And on the way I dropped it.

A little boy picked it up,

And put it in his pocket.

I Had a Little Hen

I had a little hen,
    the prettiest ever seen,
She washed up the dishes,
    and kept the house clean.

She went to the mill
    to fetch me some flour,
And always got home
    in less than an hour.

She baked me my bread,
    she brewed me my ale,
She sat by the fire
    and told a fine tale!

Little Jack Horner

Little Jack Horner sat in the corner,

Eating his Christmas pie;

He put in his thumb, and pulled out a plum,

And said, "What a good boy am I!"

Old Mother Hubbard

Old Mother Hubbard
Went to the cupboard,
To get her poor dog a bone;

But when she got there
The cupboard was bare,
And her poor dog had none.

Teddy Bear, Teddy Bear

(Do the same actions as Teddy.)

Teddy bear, teddy bear,

Touch the ground.

Teddy bear, teddy bear,

Turn around.

Teddy bear, teddy bear,

Walk upstairs.

Teddy bear, teddy bear,
Say your prayers.

Teddy bear, teddy bear,
Turn out the light.

Teddy bear, teddy bear,
Say good night.

The Grand Old Duke of York

The grand old Duke of York,

He had ten thousand men,

He marched them up to the top of the hill,

And he marched them down again.

When they were up, they were up,

And when they were down, they were down,

And when they were only halfway up,

They were neither up nor down.

Jack
Be
Nimble

Jack be nimble,

Jack be quick,

Jack jump over

The candlestick.

Little Nancy Etticoat

Little Nancy Etticoat,

In a white petticoat,

And a red rose.

The longer she stands,

The shorter she grows.

What is she?

(Riddle answer: A candle)

Georgie Porgie

Georgie Porgie, pudding, and pie,

Kissed the girls, and made them cry.

When the boys came out to play,

Georgie Porgie ran away.

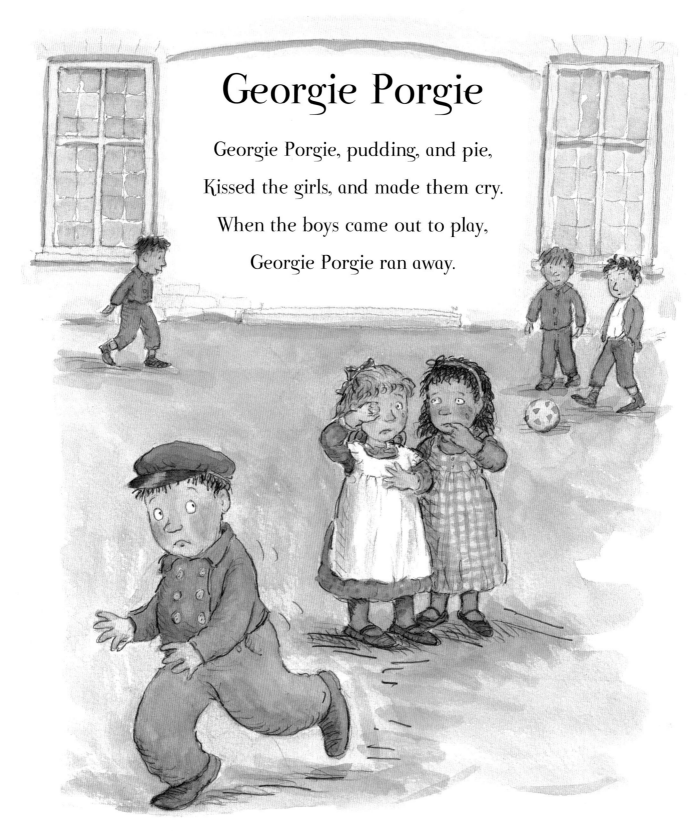

One Misty, Moisty Morning

One misty, moisty morning,

When cloudy was the weather;

There I met an old man

Clothed all in leather,

With whiskers on his chin.

How do you do?

And how do you do?

And how do you do

AGAIN?

Ring-a-Ring
o' Roses

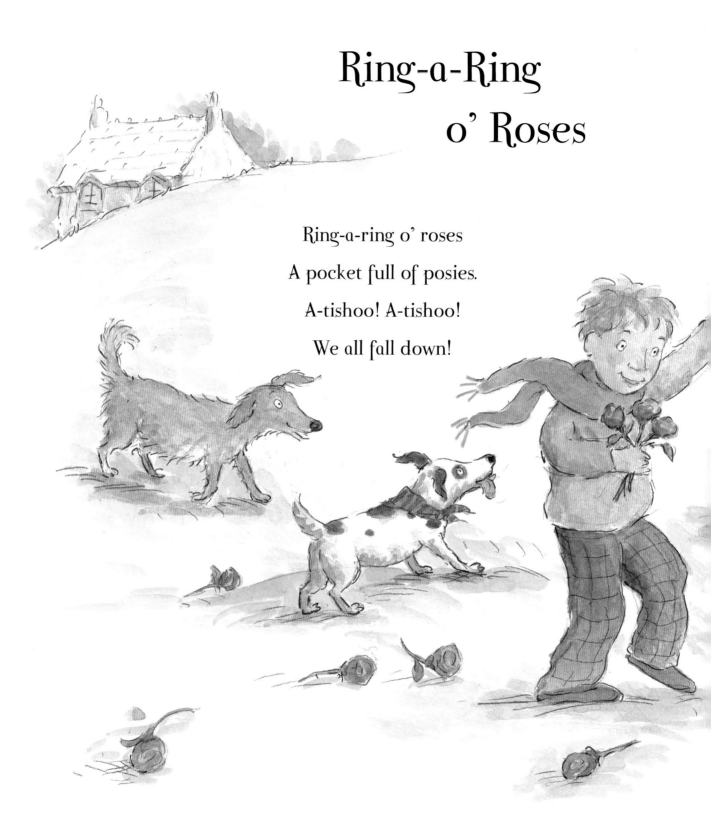

Ring-a-ring o' roses
A pocket full of posies.
A-tishoo! A-tishoo!
We all fall down!

As I Was Going to St. Ives

As I was going to St. Ives,

I met a man with seven wives.

Each wife had seven sacks;

Each sack had seven cats;

Each cat had seven kits.

Kits, cats, sacks, and wives.

How many were going to St. Ives?

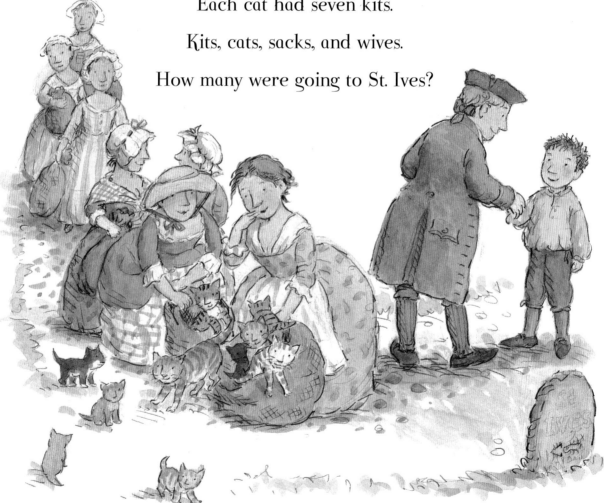

(Riddle answer: Just one person is going to St. Ives—I.)

Eeny, Meeny

Eeny, meeny, miney, mo,

Catch a tiger by the toe,

If he hollers let him go,

Eeny, meeny, miney, mo.

Horsey, Horsey

Horsey, horsey, don't you stop,

Just let your feet go clippety clop;

Your tail goes swish,

And the wheels go round;

Giddy-up, you're homeward bound!

Sing a Song of Sixpence

Sing a song of sixpence
    A pocket full of rye;
Four and twenty blackbirds
    Baked in a pie.
When the pie was opened,
    The birds began to sing;
Now wasn't that a dainty dish
    To set before the king?

The king was in his counting house,
    Counting out his money;
The queen was in the parlour
    Eating bread and honey.
The maid was in the garden
    Hanging out the clothes,
When down came a blackbird
    And pecked off her nose!

I Had a Little Puppy

I had a little puppy,

His name was Tiny Tim.

I put him in the bathtub,

To see if he could swim.

He drank up all the water,

He ate a bar of soap.

The next thing you know

He had a bubble in his throat.

In came the doctor,

In came the nurse,

In came the lady with the alligator purse.

Out went the doctor,

Out went the nurse,

Out went the lady with the alligator purse.

Humpty Dumpty

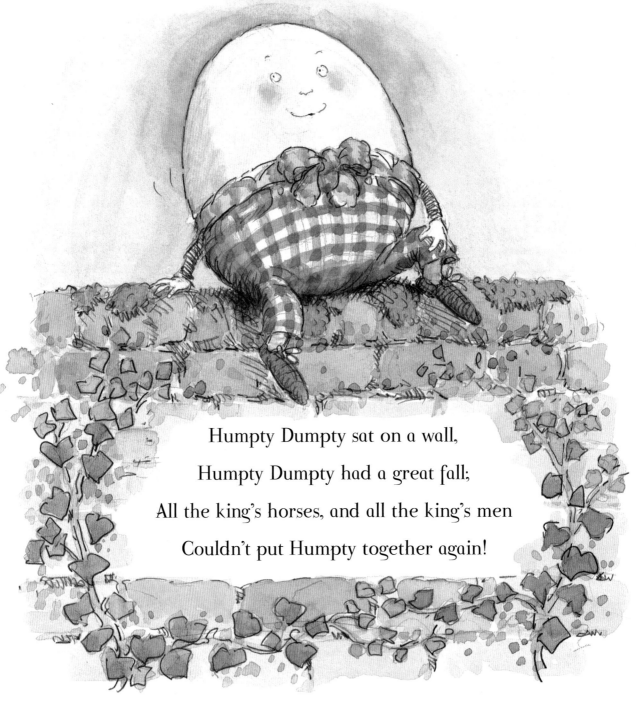

Humpty Dumpty sat on a wall,

Humpty Dumpty had a great fall;

All the king's horses, and all the king's men

Couldn't put Humpty together again!

There Was a Little Girl

There was a little girl,
And she had a little curl,
Right in the middle
Of her forehead.

When she was good,
She was very, very good,
But when she was bad,
She was HORRID.

Little Miss Muffet

Little Miss Muffet
Sat on a tuffet,
Eating her curds and whey;

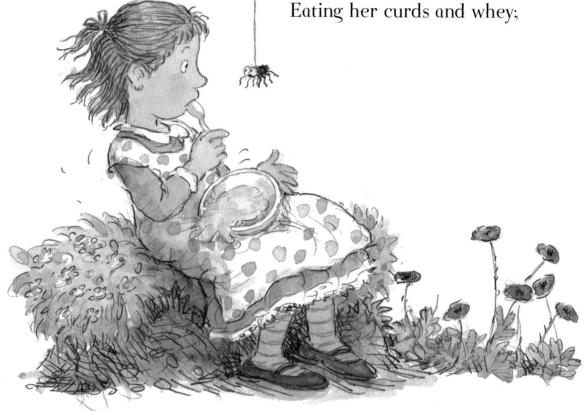

Along came a spider,

Who sat down beside her

And frightened Miss Muffet away.

See-Saw, Margery Daw

See-saw, Margery Daw,

Johnny shall have a new master;

He shall have but a penny a day,

Because he can't work any faster.

Tom, Tom, the Piper's Son

Tom, Tom, the piper's son,

Stole a pig and away he ran.

The pig was eat, and Tom was beat,

And Tom went roaring down the street.

Monday's Child

Monday's child is fair of face,

Tuesday's child is full of grace,

Wednesday's child is full of woe,

Thursday's child has far to go,

Friday's child is loving and giving,

Saturday's child works hard for his living,

And the child that is born on the Sabbath day

Is bonny and blithe, and good, and gay.

Coffee and Tea

Molly, my sister, and I fell out,

And what do you think it was all about?

She loved coffee and I loved tea,

And that was the reason we couldn't agree.

Two Little Dickie Birds

Two little dickie birds sitting on a wall,

One named Peter, one named Paul.

Fly away Peter, fly away Paul,

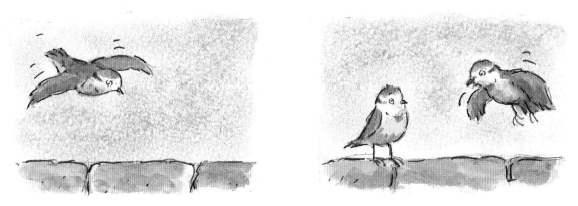

Come back Peter, come back Paul!

Jack and Jill

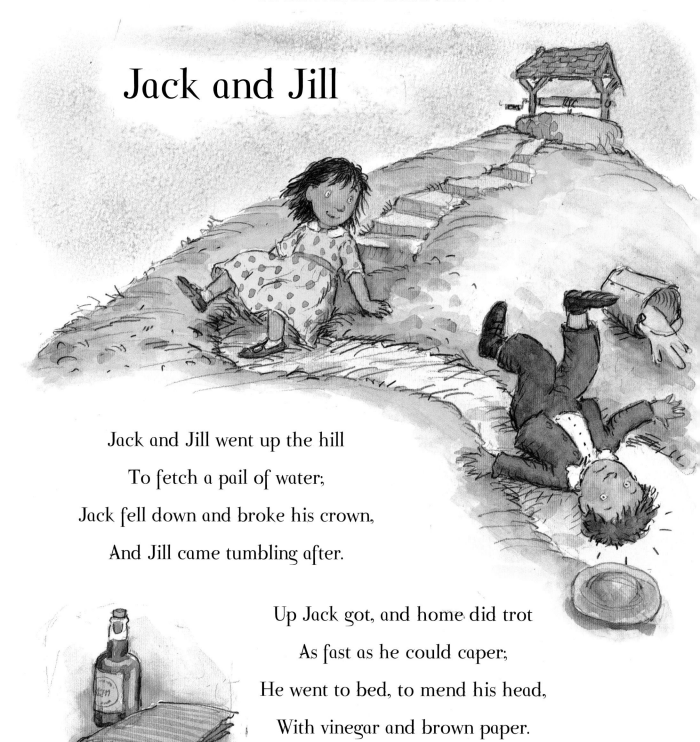

Jack and Jill went up the hill
To fetch a pail of water;
Jack fell down and broke his crown,
And Jill came tumbling after.

Up Jack got, and home did trot
As fast as he could caper;
He went to bed, to mend his head,
With vinegar and brown paper.

One Potato, Two Potato

One potato,

Two potato,

Three potato,

Four.

Five potato,

Six potato,

Seven potato,

MORE!

A was an Apple Pie

A was an apple pie,

B bit it,

C cut it,

D dealt it,

E eat it,

F fought for it,

G got it,

H had it,

I inspected it,

J jumped for it,

K kept it,

L longed for it,

M mourned for it,

N nodded at it,

O opened it,

P peeked in it,

Q quartered it,

R ran for it,

S stole it,

T took it,

U upset it,

V viewed it,

W wanted it,

X, Y, Z,

All wished for

a piece in hand.

Lavender's Blue

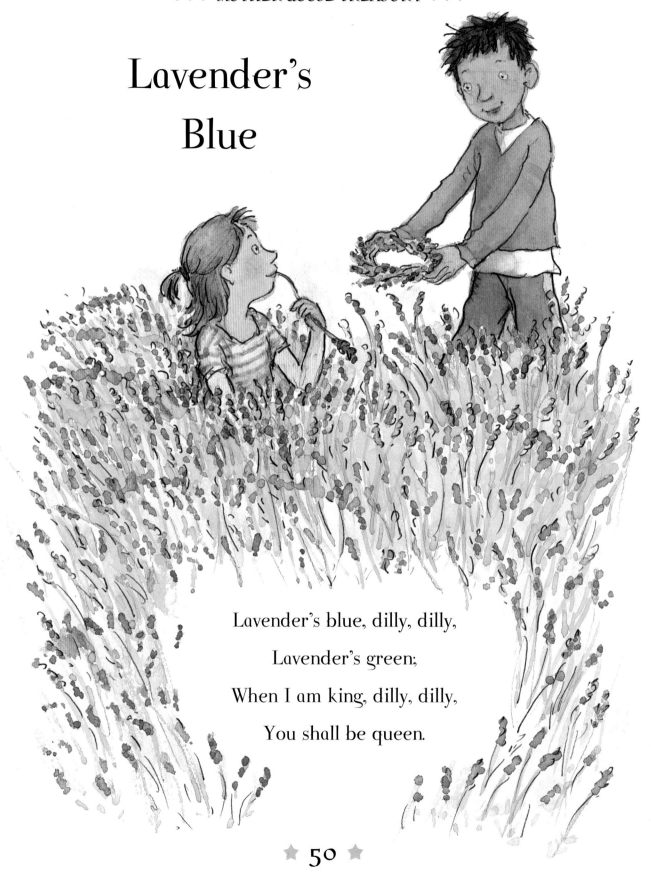

Lavender's blue, dilly, dilly,
Lavender's green;
When I am king, dilly, dilly,
You shall be queen.

Five Fat Peas

Five fat peas in a pea-pod pressed,

One grew, two grew, so did all the rest.

They grew, and grew, and did not stop,

Until one day,

the pod went POP!

One for Sorrow

One for sorrow,

Two for joy,

Three for a girl,

Four for a boy,

Five for silver,

Six for gold,

Seven for a secret

Never to be told.

Pat-a-Cake, Pat-a-Cake

Pat-a-cake, pat-a-cake, baker's man,

(Clap in rhythm)

Bake me a cake as fast as you can.

(Pat and "prick" palm)

Pat it and prick it and mark it with B,

(Trace the letter B on palm)

And put it in the oven for Baby and me!

(Action of putting cake in oven)

There Was an Old Woman Who Lived in a Shoe

There was an old woman
who lived in a shoe.
She had so many children
she didn't know what to do!
So she gave them some broth
without any bread;
And she scolded them soundly
and sent them to bed.

Ride a Cock-Horse

Ride a cock-horse to Banbury Cross

To see a fine lady upon a white horse.

With rings on her fingers and bells on her toes,

She shall have music wherever she goes.

Rub-a-Dub-Dub

Rub-a-dub-dub,

Three men in a tub,

And how do you think they got there?

The butcher, the baker,

The candlestick maker,

They all jumped out

    of a rotten potato,

It was enough to make

    a man stare.

I Hear Thunder

I hear thunder, I hear thunder,

Hark, don't you? Hark, don't you?

Pitter patter raindrops,

Pitter-patter raindrops,

I'm wet through,

So are you.

Solomon Grundy

Solomon Grundy,
Born on a Monday,
Christened on Tuesday,

Married on Wednesday,
Took ill on Thursday,
Grew worse on Friday,

Died on Saturday,
Buried on Sunday.
That was the end of
Solomon Grundy.

I'm a Little Teapot

I'm a little teapot, short and stout,

Here is my handle, here is my spout.

When I get all steamed up hear me shout,

Tip me over and pour me out.

Polly, Put the Kettle On

Polly, put the kettle on,

Polly, put the kettle on,

Polly, put the kettle on,

We'll all have tea.

Sukey, take it off again,

Sukey, take it off again,

Sukey, take it off again,

They've all gone away.

One, Two, Three, Four, Five

One, two, three, four, five,

Once I caught a fish alive.

Six, seven, eight, nine, ten,

Then I let it go again.

Why did you let it go?

Because it bit my finger so.

Which finger did it bite?

This little finger on the right.

Five Little Ducks

Five little ducks went swimming one day,

Over the hills and far away.

Mother duck said, "Quack, quack, quack, quack,"

But only four little ducks came back.

Four little ducks went swimming one day,

Over the hills and far away.

Mother duck said, "Quack, quack, quack, quack,"

But only three little ducks came back.

Three little ducks went swimming one day,

Over the hills and far away.

Mother duck said, "Quack, quack, quack, quack,"

But only two little ducks came back.

Two little ducks went swimming one day,

Over the hills and far away.

Mother duck said, "Quack, quack, quack, quack,"

But only one little duck came back.

One little duck went swimming one day,

Over the hills and far away.

Mother duck said, "Quack, quack, quack, quack,"

But none of the five little ducks came back.

Mother duck went swimming one day,

Over the hills and far away.

Mother duck said, "Quack, quack, quack, quack,"

And five little ducks came swimming back.

Old King Cole

Old King Cole was a merry old soul,

And a merry old soul was he;

He called for his pipe, and he called for his bowl,

And he called for his fiddlers three.

Every fiddler had a very fine fiddle,

And a very fine fiddle had he;

Oh, there's none so rare as can compare

With King Cole and his fiddlers three.

The Incy Wincy Spider

The incy wincy spider climbed up the water spout,

(Use your fingers to show the spider climbing up the spout.)

Down came the rain and washed the spider out.

(Wiggle your fingers to show the rain.)

Out came the sun, and dried up all the rain,

(Make a big circle with your arms.)

And the incy wincy spider climbed up the spout again.

(Repeat the action for the first line.)

Hector Protector

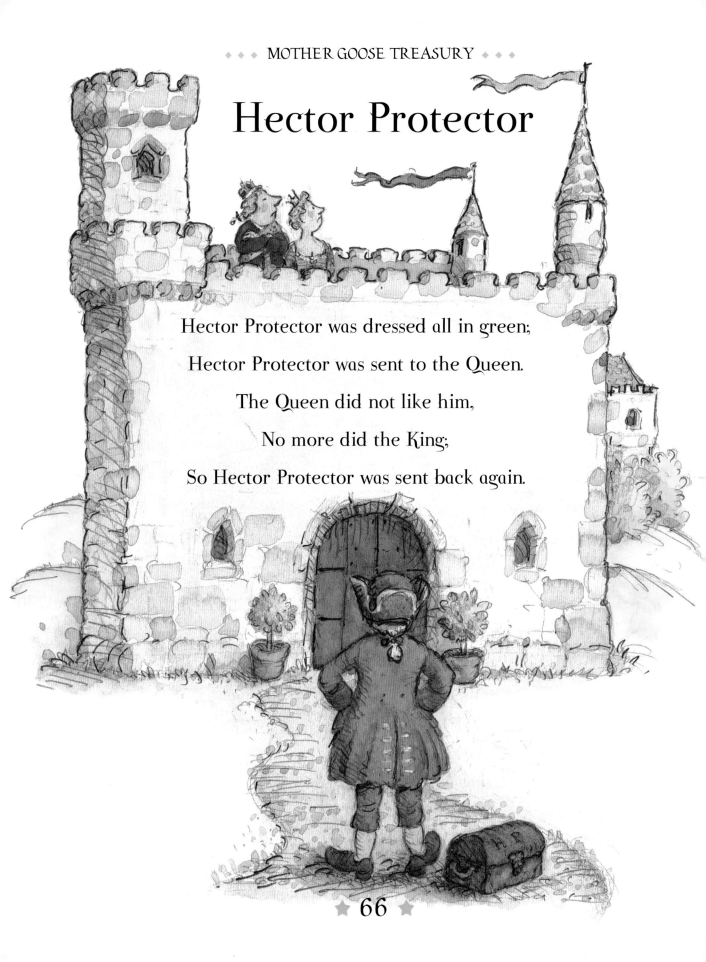

Hector Protector was dressed all in green;

Hector Protector was sent to the Queen.

The Queen did not like him,

No more did the King;

So Hector Protector was sent back again.

Row, Row, Row Your Boat

(Mime a rowing action throughout, as the rhyme suggests.)

Row, row, row your boat

Gently down the stream.

Merrily, merrily, merrily, merrily,

Life is but a dream.

To Market, To Market

To market, to market, to buy a fat pig,

Home again, home again, jiggety-jig;

To market, to market, to buy a fat hog,

Home again, home again, jiggety-jog.

To market, to market, to buy a plum cake,

Home again, home again, market is late;

To market, to market, to buy a plum bun,

Home again, home again, market is done.

Cobbler, Cobbler, Mend my Shoe

Cobbler, cobbler, mend my shoe.

Get it done by half past two.

Half past two is much too late!

Get it done by half past eight.

Lucy Locket

Lucy Locket lost her pocket,

Kitty Fisher found it.

Not a penny was there in it,

Only ribbon round it.

Tinker, Tailor, Soldier, Sailor

Tinker,

Tailor,

Soldier,

Sailor,

Rich man,

Poor man,

Beggarman,

Thief!

Five Fat Sausages

Five fat sausages sizzling in the pan,

All of a sudden one went BANG!

Four fat sausages sizzling in the pan,

All of a sudden one went BANG!

Three fat sausages sizzling in the pan,

All of a sudden one went BANG!

Two fat sausages sizzling in the pan,

All of a sudden one went BANG!

One fat sausage sizzling in the pan,

All of a sudden it went BANG!

And there were no sausages left!

Round and Round the Garden

Round and round the garden

Like a teddy bear;

(Draw a circle on the palm of your baby's hand

with your finger.)

One step, two steps,

("Walk" your fingers up your baby's arm.)

Tickle you under there!

(Tickle baby under the arm.)

Each Peach, Pear, Plum

Each peach, pear, plum,

Out goes Tom Thumb;

Tom Thumb won't do,

Out goes Betty Blue;

Betty Blue won't go,

So out goes you.

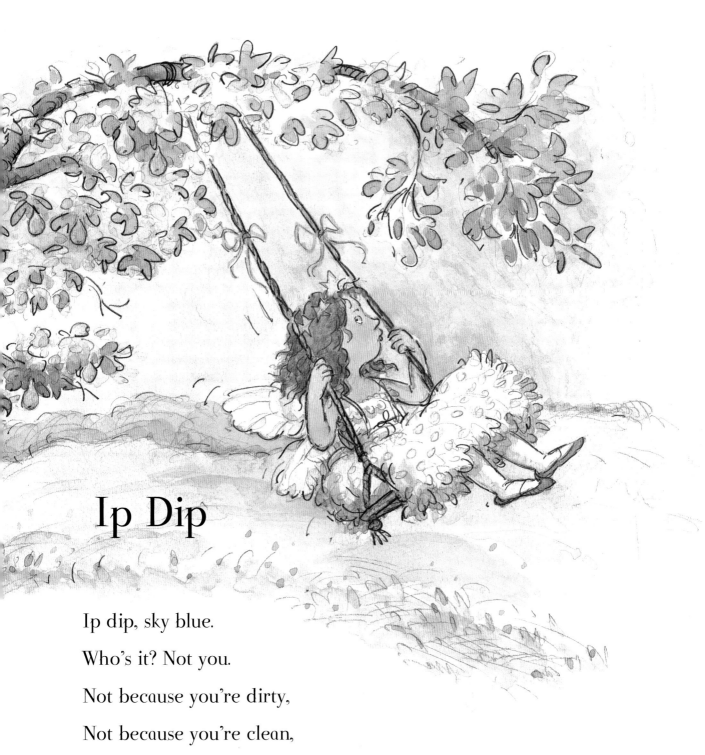

Ip Dip

Ip dip, sky blue.

Who's it? Not you.

Not because you're dirty,

Not because you're clean,

My mother says you're the fairy queen.

This Old Man

This old man, he played one;

He played knick-knack on my thumb.

    Chorus: With a knick-knack, paddy whack,

                     Give a dog a bone;

                     This old man came rolling home.

This old man, he played two;

He played knick-knack on my shoe.

    Chorus: With a knick-knack, paddy whack,

                     Give a dog a bone;

                     This old man came rolling home.

This old man, he played three;

He played knick-knack on my knee.

Chorus: With a knick-knack, paddy whack,

Give a dog a bone;

This old man came rolling home.

This old man, he played four;

He played knick-knack on my door.

Chorus: With a knick-knack, paddy whack,

Give a dog a bone;

This old man came rolling home.

This old man, he played five;

He played knick-knack on my hive.

Chorus: With a knick-knack, paddy whack,

Give a dog a bone;

This old man came rolling home.

This old man, he played six;

He played knick-knack on my sticks.

  Chorus: With a knick-knack, paddy whack,

      Give a dog a bone;

      This old man came rolling home.

This old man, he played seven;

He played knick-knack up to heaven.

  Chorus

This old man, he played eight;

He played knick-knack on my gate.

  Chorus

This old man, he played nine;

He played knick-knack on my spine.

  Chorus

This old man, he played ten;

He played knick-knack once again.

  Chorus

Here Is the Church

Here is the church,

(Interlace fingers.)

Here is the steeple,

(Put up both pointing fingers to make a steeple.)

Look inside...

(Turn both hands over.)

And see all the people!

(Wiggle your fingers.)

Mary, Mary, Quite Contrary

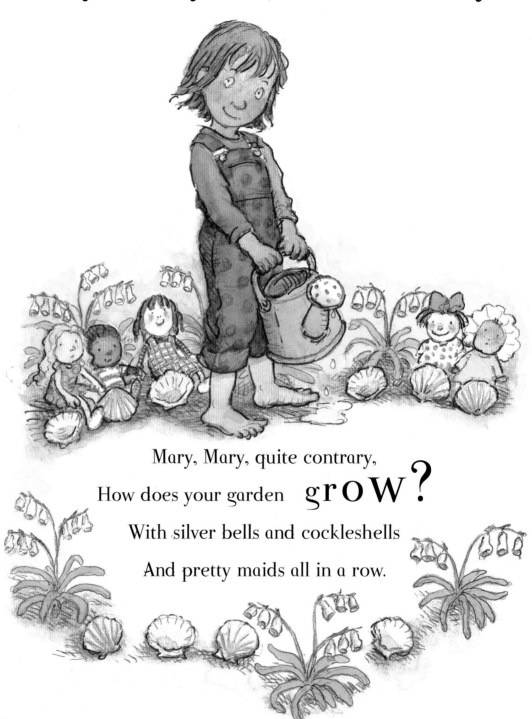

Mary, Mary, quite contrary,

How does your garden grOW?

With silver bells and cockleshells

And pretty maids all in a row.

Hot Cross Buns!

Hot cross buns!

Hot cross buns!

One a penny, two a penny,

Hot cross buns!

If you have no daughters,

Give them to your sons.

One a penny, two a penny,

Hot cross buns!

One Man Went to Mow

One man went to mow,

Went to mow a meadow,

One man, and his dog,

Went to mow a meadow.

Two men went to mow,

Went to mow a meadow,

Two men, one man, and his dog,

Went to mow a meadow.

Three men went to mow,

Went to mow a meadow,

Three men, two men,

one man, and his dog,

Went to mow a meadow.

Four men went to mow,

Went to mow a meadow,

Four men, three men, two men,

one man, and his dog,

Went to mow a meadow.

You can keep adding verses as far as you can count.

Five Little Monkeys

Five little monkeys jumping on the bed,

One fell off and bumped his head.

Mum called the doctor and the doctor said,

"No more monkeys jumping on the bed!"

Four little monkeys jumping on the bed,

One fell off and bumped her head.

Dad called the doctor and the doctor said,

"No more monkeys jumping on the bed!"

Three little monkeys jumping on the bed,

One fell off and bumped his head.

Mum called the doctor and the doctor said,

"No more monkeys jumping on the bed!"

Two little monkeys jumping on the bed,

One fell off and bumped her head.

Dad called the doctor and the doctor said,

"No more monkeys jumping on the bed!"

One little monkey jumping on the bed,

He fell off and bumped his head.

Mum called the doctor and the doctor said,

"Put those monkeys straight to bed!"

Catch It if You Can

Mix a pancake,

Beat a pancake,

Put it in a pan.

Cook a pancake,

Toss a pancake,

Catch it if you can!

Do You Know
the Muffin Man?

Oh, do you know the muffin man,

The muffin man, the muffin man?

Oh, do you know the muffin man,

That lives on Drury Lane?

Oh yes, I know the muffin man,

The muffin man, the muffin man!

Oh yes, I know the muffin man,

That lives on Drury Lane!

This Is the Way

This is the way we wash our hands,
Wash our hands, wash our hands.
This is the way we wash our hands
So early in the morning.

This is the way we wash our face,
Wash our face, wash our face.
This is the way we wash our face
So early in the morning.

This is the way we brush our teeth,

Brush our teeth, brush our teeth.

This is the way we brush our teeth

So early in the morning.

This is the way we brush our hair,

Brush our hair, brush our hair.

This is the way we brush our hair

So early in the morning.

This is the way we wave goodbye,

Wave goodbye, wave goodbye.

This is the way we wave goodbye

So early in the morning.

One, Two, Buckle my Shoe

One, two, buckle my shoe;

Three, four, knock at the door;

Five, six, pick up sticks;

Seven, eight, lay them straight;

Nine, ten, a big fat hen;

Eleven, twelve, dig and delve;

Thirteen, fourteen, maids a-courting;

Fifteen, sixteen, maids in the kitchen;

Seventeen, eighteen, maids in waiting;

Nineteen, twenty, my plate's empty!

Jack Sprat

Jack Sprat could eat no fat,

His wife could eat no lean;

And so, between the two of them,

They licked the platter clean.

Pease Porridge Hot

Pease porridge hot, pease porridge cold,

Pease porridge in the pot, nine days old.

Some like it hot, some like it cold,

Some like it in the pot, nine days old.

An Elephant Walks

An elephant walks like this and that;

He's terribly tall and he's terribly fat.

He's got no fingers,

He's got no toes,

But goodness gracious,

What a long, long nose!

Peter, Peter

Peter, Peter, pumpkin eater,

Had a wife and couldn't keep her.

He put her in a pumpkin shell

And there he kept her very well.

Mary Had a Little Lamb

Mary had a little lamb,

Its fleece was white as snow;

And everywhere that Mary went

The lamb was sure to go.

It followed her to school one day,

Which was against the rule;

It made the children laugh and play

To see a lamb at school.

Doctor Foster

Doctor Foster

Went to Gloucester

In a shower of rain;

He stepped in a puddle,

Right up to his middle,

And never went there again!

Simple Simon

Simple Simon met a pieman going to the fair;

Said Simple Simon to the pieman,

"Let me taste your ware."

Said the pieman to Simple Simon,

"Show me first your penny."

Said Simple Simon to the pieman,

"Sir, I have not any!"

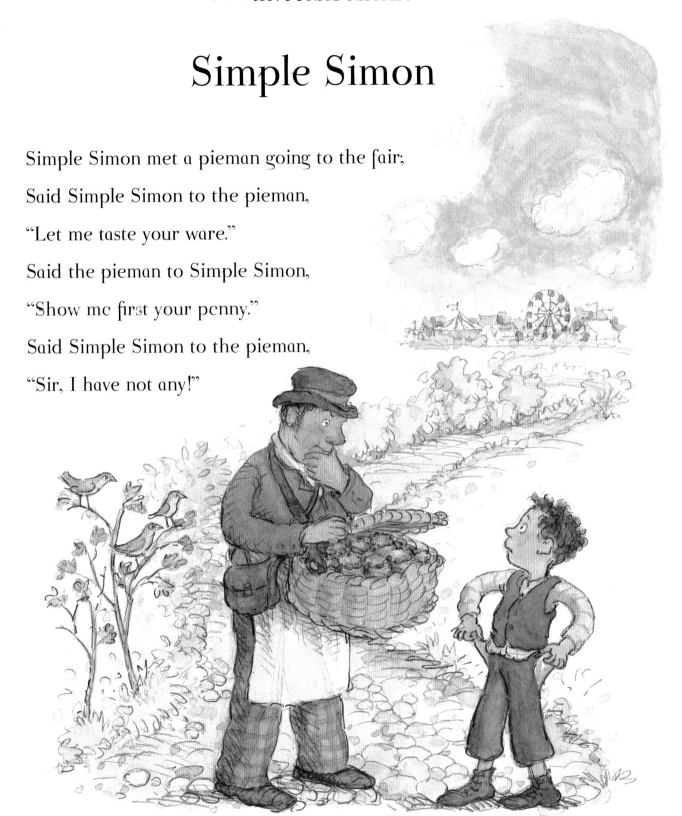

This Little Piggy

(Pretend each of the child's toes is a little piggy.
Begin with the biggest toe and finish by tickling under the child's foot.)

This little piggy

went to market,

This little piggy

stayed home,

This little piggy
had roast beef,

This little piggy
had none,

And this little piggy cried,
"Wee, wee, wee!"
All the way home.

Baa, Baa, Black Sheep

Baa, baa, black sheep,

Have you any wool?

Yes sir, yes sir,

Three bags full.

One for the master,

And one for the dame,

And one for the little boy

Who lives down the lane.

Pussy Cat, Pussy Cat

Pussy cat, pussy cat,

Where have you been?

I've been to London

To visit the Queen.

Pussy cat, pussy cat,

What did you there?

I frightened a little mouse

Under her chair.

The Wheels on the Bus

The wheels on the bus go

round and round,

Round and round,

round and round.

The wheels on the bus go

round and round,

All day long.

(Move hands in a circular motion.)

The wipers on the bus go

swish, swish, swish!

Swish, swish, swish!

swish, swish, swish!

The wipers on the bus go

swish, swish, swish!

All day long.

(Wiggle both index fingers.)

The horn on the bus goes

beep, beep, beep!

Beep, beep, beep!

beep, beep, beep!

The horn on the bus goes

beep, beep, beep!

All day long.

(Pretend to press a horn.)

The people on the bus go

chatter, chatter, chatter,

Chatter, chatter, chatter,

chatter, chatter, chatter.

The people on the bus go

chatter, chatter, chatter,

All day long.

Little Tommy Tucker

Little Tommy Tucker sings for his supper.

What shall we give him? Brown bread and butter.

How shall he cut it without a knife?

How shall he marry without a wife?

Cock-a-Doodle-Doo!

Cock-a-doodle-doo!

My dame has lost her shoe!

My master's lost his fiddling stick,

And doesn't know what to do.

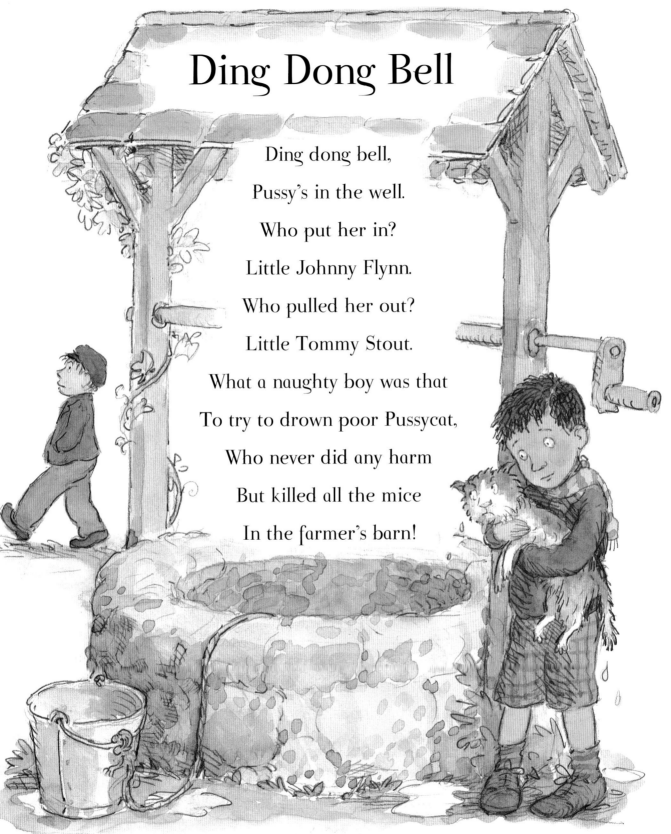

Ding Dong Bell

Ding dong bell,

Pussy's in the well.

Who put her in?

Little Johnny Flynn.

Who pulled her out?

Little Tommy Stout.

What a naughty boy was that

To try to drown poor Pussycat,

Who never did any harm

But killed all the mice

In the farmer's barn!

Rain, Rain, Go Away

Rain, rain, go away,

Come again another day.

Little Johnny wants to play.

Oats, Peas, Beans, and Barley Grow

Oats, peas, beans, and barley grow,

Oats, peas, beans, and barley grow.

Can you or I or anyone know

How oats, peas, beans, and barley grow?

First the farmer sows his seed,

Then he stands and takes his ease.

Stamps his feet and claps his hands,

And turns around to view his lands.

Oats, peas, beans, and barley grow,

Oats, peas, beans, and barley grow.

Can you or I or anyone know

How oats, peas, beans, and barley grow?

Goosey, Goosey, Gander

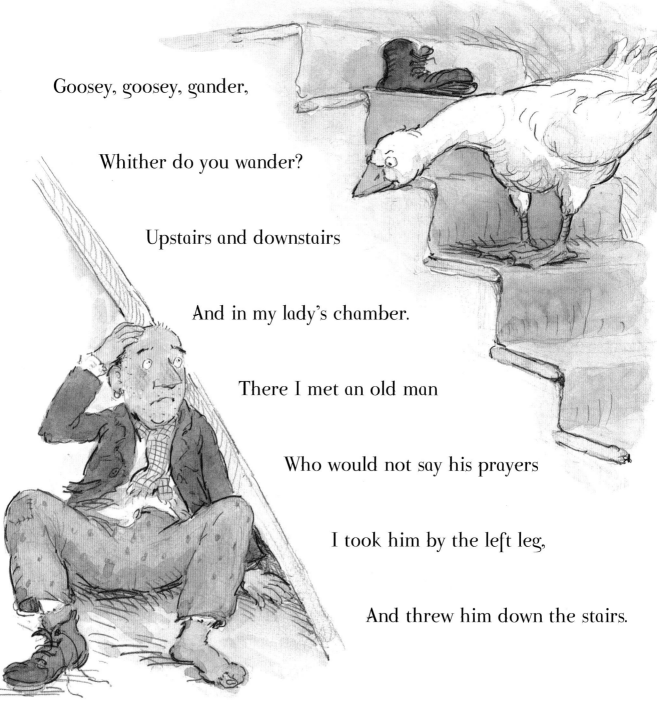

Goosey, goosey, gander,

Whither do you wander?

Upstairs and downstairs

And in my lady's chamber.

There I met an old man

Who would not say his prayers

I took him by the left leg,

And threw him down the stairs.

Hickory, Dickory, Dock

Hickory, dickory, dock,

The mouse ran up the clock.

The clock struck one,

The mouse ran down,

Hickory, dickory, dock.

Little Robin Redbreast

Little Robin Redbreast sat upon a tree,

Up went Pussycat, and down went he!

Down came Pussy, and away Robin ran;

Said little Robin Redbreast,

"Catch me if you can!"

Meow

Little Robin Redbreast

flew upon a wall,

Pussycat jumped after him,

and almost had a fall!

Little Robin chirped and sang,

and what did Pussy say?

Pussy cat said, "Meow,"

and Robin flew away.

I Had a Little Hobby-Horse

I had a little hobby-horse,

And it was dapple grey;

Its head was made of pea-straw,

Its tail was made of hay.

I sold it to an old woman

For a copper groat;

And I'll not sing my song again

Without another coat.

Twinkle, Twinkle, Little Star

Twinkle, twinkle, little star,
How I wonder what you are!
Up above the world so high,
Like a diamond in the sky.

When the blazing sun is gone,
When he nothing shines upon,
Then you show your little light,
Twinkle, twinkle all the night.

Then the traveller in the dark,

Thanks you for your tiny spark,

He could not see which way to go,

If you did not twinkle so.

In the dark blue sky you keep,

And often through my curtains peep,

For you never shut your eye,

Till the sun is in the sky.

As your bright and tiny spark,

Lights the traveller in the dark—

Though I know not what you are,

Twinkle, twinkle, little star.

—Jane Taylor

Betty Botter Bought Some Butter

Betty Botter bought some butter,

But she said, "The butter's bitter.

If I put it in my batter,

It will make my batter bitter.

But a bit of better butter

Will make my batter better."

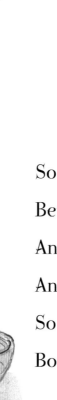

So she bought some better butter,

Better than the bitter butter,

And she put it in her batter.

And her batter was not bitter.

So 'twas better Betty Botter

Bought a bit of better butter.

It's Raining, It's Pouring

It's raining, it's pouring,

The old man is snoring.

He went to bed and he bumped his head,

And couldn't get up in the morning.

Hickety Pickety

Hickety Pickety, my black hen,

She lays eggs for gentlemen;

Sometimes nine, and sometimes ten,

Hickety Pickety, my black hen!

Pop Goes the Weasel

Half a pound of tuppenny rice,

Half a pound of treacle.

That's the way the money goes,

Pop goes the weasel!

Up and down the city road,

In and out the Eagle,

That's the way the money goes,

Pop goes the weasel!

Hey Diddle Diddle

Hey diddle diddle, the cat and the fiddle,

The cow jumped over the moon.

The little dog laughed to see such fun

And the dish ran away with the spoon!

Three Blind Mice

Three blind mice, three blind mice,

See how they run, see how they run!

They all ran after the farmer's wife,

Who cut off their tails with a carving knife,

Did you ever see such a thing in your life

As three blind mice?

Go to Bed First

Go to bed first,

A golden purse;

Go to bed second,

A golden pheasant;

Go to bed third,

A golden bird.

Higglety, Pigglety, Pop!

Higglety, pigglety, pop!

The dog has eaten the mop;

The pig's in a hurry,

The cat's in a flurry,

Higglety, pigglety, POP!

Sippity Sup, Sippity Sup

Sippity sup, sippity sup,

Bread and milk from a china cup.

Bread and milk from a bright silver spoon

Made of a piece of the bright silver moon.

Sippity sup, sippity sup,

Sippity, sippity sup.

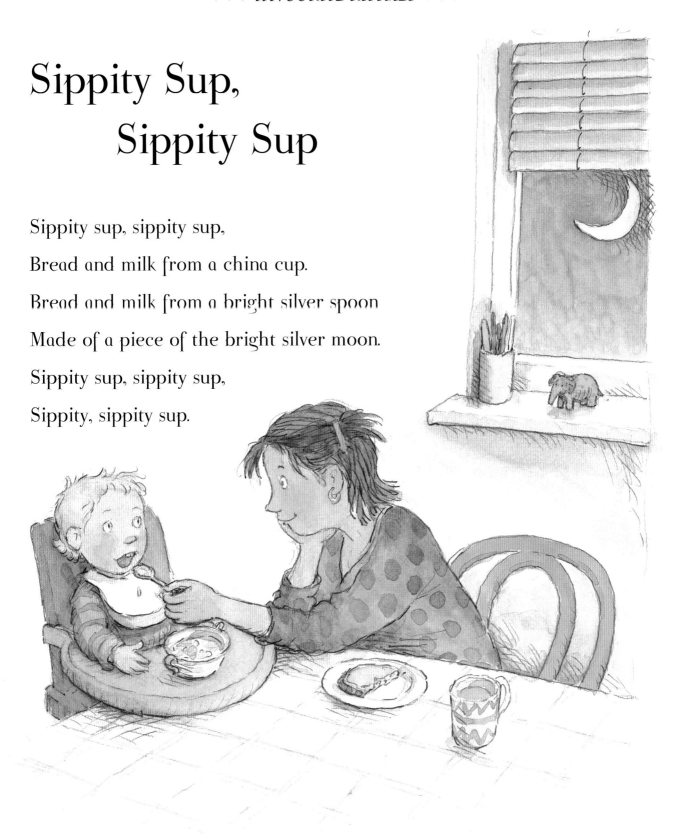

The Owl and the Pussycat

The Owl and the Pussycat went to sea

In a beautiful pea-green boat,

They took some honey, and plenty of money,

Wrapped up in a five pound note.

The Owl looked up to the stars above,

And sang to a small guitar,

"Oh lovely Pussy! Oh Pussy, my love,

What a beautiful Pussy you are, you are, you are,

What a beautiful Pussy you are."

Pussy said to the Owl, "You elegant fowl,

How charmingly sweet you sing.

Oh let us be married, too long we have tarried;

But what shall we do for a ring?"

They sailed away, for a year and a day,

To the land where the Bong-tree grows,

And there in a wood a Piggy-wig stood

With a ring at the end of his nose, his nose, his nose,

With a ring at the end of his nose.

"Dear Pig, are you willing to sell for one shilling your ring?"

Said the Piggy, "I will."

So they took it away, and were married next day

By the Turkey who lives on the hill.

They dined on mince, and slices of quince,

Which they ate with a runcible spoon.

And hand in hand, on the edge of the sand,

They danced by the light of the moon, the moon, the moon,

They danced by the light of the moon.

—Edward Lear

Golden Slumbers

Golden slumbers kiss your eyes,

Smiles await you when you rise;

Sleep, pretty baby, do not cry,

And I will sing a lullaby.

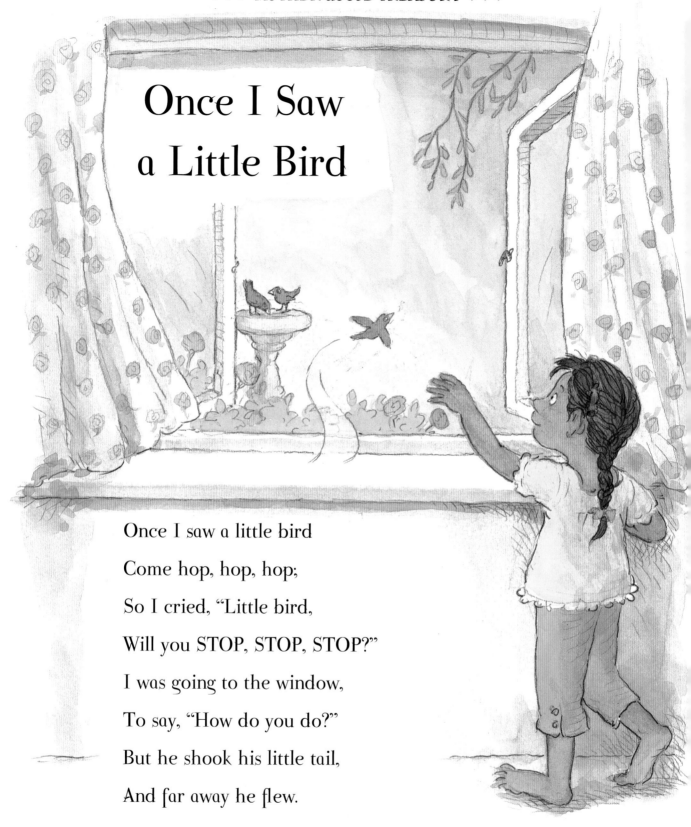

Once I Saw a Little Bird

Once I saw a little bird

Come hop, hop, hop;

So I cried, "Little bird,

Will you STOP, STOP, STOP?"

I was going to the window,

To say, "How do you do?"

But he shook his little tail,

And far away he flew.

Now the Day is Over

Now the day is over,

Night is drawing nigh,

Shadows of the evening

Steal across the sky.

Now the darkness gathers,

Stars begins to peep,

Birds and beasts and flowers

Soon will be asleep.

—Sabine Baring-Gould

What Are Little Boys Made Of?

What are little boys made of?

What are little boys made of?

Snips and snails,

And puppy-dogs' tails,

That's what little boys are made of.

What Are Little Girls Made Of?

What are little girls made of?

What are little girls made of?

Sugar and spice,

And all things nice,

That's what little girls are made of.

Aiken Drum

There was a man lived in the moon,

Lived in the moon, lived in the moon,

There was a man lived in the moon,

And his name was Aiken Drum.

And he played upon a ladle,

A ladle, a ladle,

And he played upon a ladle,

And his name was Aiken Drum.

And his hat was made of good cream cheese,

Good cream cheese, good cream cheese,

And his hat was made of good cream cheese,

And his name was Aiken Drum.

And his coat was made of good roast beef,

Good roast beef, good roast beef,

And his coat was made of good roast beef,

And his name was Aiken Drum.

And his buttons were made of penny loaves,

Penny loaves, penny loaves,

And his buttons were made of penny loaves,

And his name was Aiken Drum.

And his breeches were made of haggis bags,

Haggis bags, Haggis bags.

And his breeches were made of haggis bags,

And his name was Aiken Drum.

Diddle Diddle Dumpling

Diddle, diddle, dumpling, my son John,

Went to bed with his breeches on;

One shoe off, and the other shoe on,

Diddle, diddle, dumpling, my son John.

Robin and Richard

Robin and Richard were two pretty men,

They lay in bed till the clock struck ten;

Then up starts Robin, and looks at the sky,

"Oh! Oh! Brother Richard, the sun's very high!

You go before with bottle and bag,

And I'll follow after on little Jack Nag."

Brahms's Lullaby

Lullaby, and good night,

With roses bedight,

With lilies overspread,

Is my baby's sweet bed.

Lay you down now, and rest,

May your slumber be blessed!

Lay you down now, and rest,

May your slumber be blessed!

Lullaby, and good night,

You're your mother's delight.

Shining angels beside

My darling abide.

Soft and warm is your bed,

Close your eyes and rest your head.

Soft and warm is your bed,

Close your eyes and rest your head.

Intery, Mintery

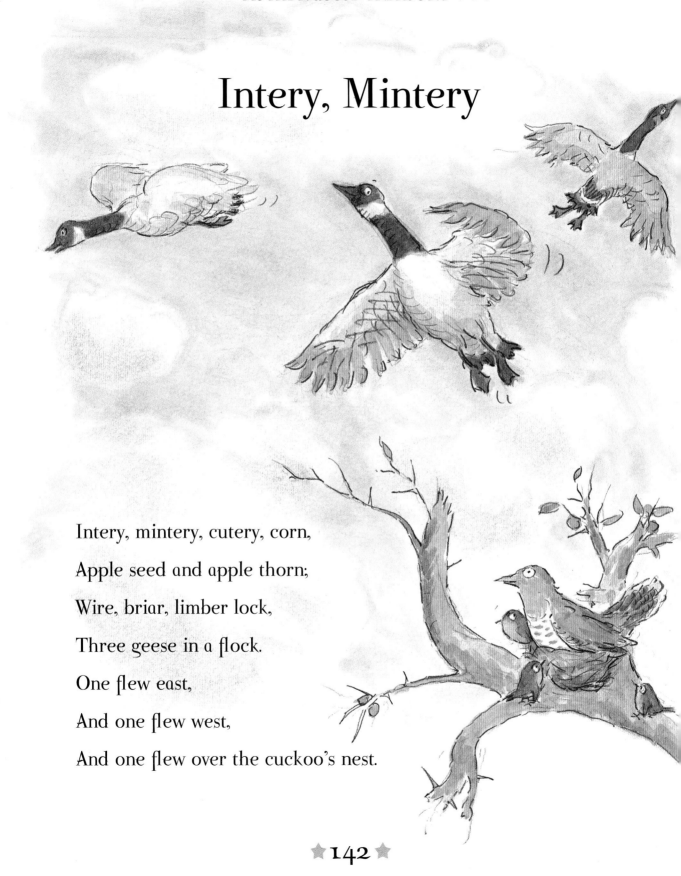

Intery, mintery, cutery, corn,

Apple seed and apple thorn;

Wire, briar, limber lock,

Three geese in a flock.

One flew east,

And one flew west,

And one flew over the cuckoo's nest.

The Lion
and the Unicorn

The lion and the unicorn were fighting for the crown;

The lion beat the unicorn all around the town.

Some gave them white bread,

And some gave them brown;

Some gave them plum cake,

And drummed them out of town.

The House that Jack Built

This is the house that Jack built.

This is the malt

That lay in the house that Jack built.

This is the rat,

That ate the malt

That lay in the house that Jack built.

This is the cat,

That killed the rat,

That ate the malt

That lay in the house that Jack built.

This is the dog,

That worried the cat,

That killed the rat,

That ate the malt

That lay in the house that Jack built.

This is the cow with the crumpled horn,

That tossed the dog,

That worried the cat,

That killed the rat,

That ate the malt

That lay in the house that Jack built.

This is the maiden all forlorn,

That milked the cow with the crumpled horn,

That tossed the dog,

That worried the cat,

That killed the rat,

That ate the malt

That lay in the house that Jack built.

This is the man all tattered and torn,

That kissed the maiden all forlorn,

That milked the cow with the crumpled horn,

That tossed the dog,

That worried the cat,

That killed the rat,

That ate the malt

That lay in the house that Jack built.

This is the priest all shaven and shorn,

That married the man all tattered and torn,

That kissed the maiden all forlorn,

That milked the cow with the crumpled horn,

That tossed the dog,

That worried the cat,

That killed the rat,

That ate the malt

That lay in the house that Jack built.

This is the cock that crowed in the morn,

That waked the priest all shaven and shorn,

That married the man all tattered and torn,

That kissed the maiden all forlorn,

That milked the cow with the crumpled horn,

That tossed the dog,

That worried the cat,

That killed the rat,

That ate the malt

That lay in the house that Jack built.

This is the farmer sowing his corn,

That kept the cock that crowed in the morn,

That waked the priest all shaven and shorn,

That married the man all tattered and torn,

That kissed the maiden all forlorn,

That milked the cow with the crumpled horn,

That tossed the dog,

That worried the cat,

That killed the rat,

That ate the malt

That lay in the house that Jack built.

The Queen of Hearts

The Queen of Hearts, she made some tarts,

All on a summer's day.

The Knave of Hearts, he stole the tarts,

And took them clean away.

The King of Hearts called for the tarts,

And beat the Knave full sore.

The Knave of Hearts brought back the tarts,

And vowed he'd steal no more.

Go to Bed Late

Go to bed late,

Stay very small;

Go to bed early,

Grow very tall.

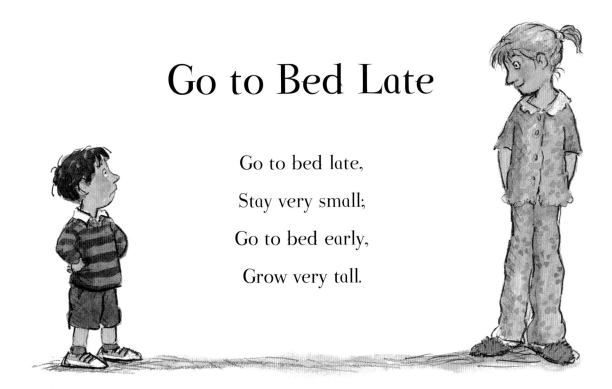

Go to Bed, Tom

Go to bed, Tom,

Go to bed, Tom,

Tired or not, Tom,

Go to bed, Tom

There Was an Old Man
Called Michael Finnegan

There was an old man called Michael Finnegan

He grew whiskers on his chinnegan.

The wind came up and blew them in again,

Poor old Michael Finnegan.

Begin again.

Bye, Baby Bunting

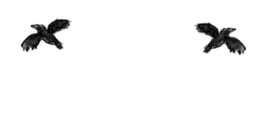

Bye, baby bunting,
Daddy's gone a-hunting,
Gone to get a rabbit-skin,
To wrap my baby bunting in.

The Farmer in the Dell

The farmer in the dell,

The farmer in the dell,

Hi-ho, the derry-o,

The farmer in the dell.

The farmer takes a wife,

The farmer takes a wife,

Hi-ho, the derry-o,

The farmer takes a wife.

The wife takes a child,

The wife takes a child,

Hi-ho, the derry-o,

The wife takes a child.

The child takes a nurse,
The child takes a nurse,
Hi-ho, the derry-o,
The child takes a nurse.

The nurse takes a dog,
The nurse takes a dog,
Hi-ho, the derry-o,
The nurse takes a dog.

The dog takes a bone,

The dog takes a bone,

Hi-ho, the derry-o,

The dog takes a bone.

We all pat the bone,

We all pat the bone,

Hi-ho, the derry-o,

We all pat the bone.

Here We Go Round the Mulberry Bush

Here we go round the mulberry bush,
The mulberry bush, the mulberry bush.
Here we go round the mulberry bush,
On a cold and frosty morning.

This is the way we wash our clothes,
Wash our clothes, wash our clothes.
This is the way we wash our clothes,
On a cold and frosty morning.

This is the way we iron our clothes,

Iron our clothes, iron our clothes.

This is the way we iron our clothes,

On a cold and frosty morning.

This is the way we scrub the floor,

Scrub the floor, scrub the floor.

This is the way we scrub the floor,

On a cold and frosty morning.

This is the way we mend our clothes,
Mend our clothes, mend our clothes.
This is the way we mend our clothes,
On a cold and frosty morning.

This is the way we sweep the floor,
Sweep the floor, sweep the floor.
This is the way we sweep the floor,
On a cold and frosty morning.

This is the way we bake our bread,

Bake our bread, bake our bread.

This is the way we bake our bread,

On a cold and frosty morning.

This is the way we get dressed up,

Get dressed up, get dressed up.

This is the way we get dressed up,

On a cold and frosty morning.

Bedtime

The evening is coming, the sun sinks to rest;

The crows are all flying straight home to the nest.

"Caw!" says the crow, as he flies overhead;

"It's time little people were going to bed!"

The flowers are closing; the daisy's asleep;

The primrose is buried in slumber so deep.

Closed for the night are the roses so red;

It's time little people were going to bed!

The butterfly, drowsy, has folded its wing;

The bees are returning, no more the birds sing.

Their labour is over, their nestlings are fed;

It's time little people were going to bed!

Oranges and Lemons

"Oranges and lemons,"

Say the bells of St. Clements.

"You owe me five farthings,"

Say the bells of St. Martins.

"When will you pay me?"

Say the bells of Old Bailey.

"When I grow rich,"

Say the bells of Shoreditch.

"When will that be?"

Say the bells of Stepney.

"I do not know,"

Says the great bell at Bow.

Here comes a candle to light you to bed,

And comes a chopper to chop off your head.

Girls and Boys

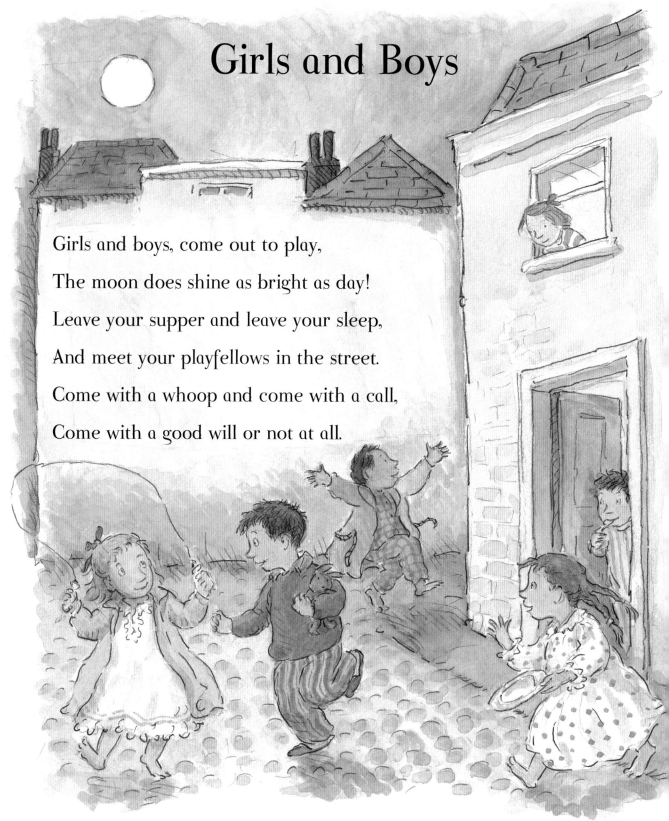

Girls and boys, come out to play,

The moon does shine as bright as day!

Leave your supper and leave your sleep,

And meet your playfellows in the street.

Come with a whoop and come with a call,

Come with a good will or not at all.

How Many Miles
to Babylon?

How many miles to Babylon?

Three score and ten.

Can I get there by candlelight?

Yes, and back again.

If your heels are nimble and light,

You may get there by candlelight.

The Big Ship Sails

The big ship sails on the ally-ally-oh,

The ally-ally-oh, the ally-ally-oh.

Oh, the big ship sails on the ally-ally-oh,

On the last day of September.

The captain said, "It will never, never do,

Never, never do, never, never do."

The captain said, "It will never, never do,"

On the last day of September.

The big ship sank to the bottom of the sea,

The bottom of the sea, the bottom of the sea.

The big ship sank to the bottom of the sea,

On the last day of September.

We all dip our hands in the deep blue sea,

The deep blue sea, the deep blue sea.

We all dip our hands in the deep blue sea

On the last day of September.

Come to Bed, Says Sleepy-Head

"Come to bed," says Sleepy-head;

"Tarry a while," says Slow;

"Put on the pot," says Greedy-gut,

"Let's sup before we go."

Wee Willie Winkie

Wee Willie Winkie

Runs through the town,

Upstairs and downstairs

In his nightgown.

Rapping at the window,

Crying through the lock,

"Are the children all in bed?

It's past eight o'clock."

A Sailor Went to Sea

A sailor went to sea, sea, sea

To see what he could see, see, see.

But all that he could see, see, see

Was the bottom of the deep blue sea, sea, sea.

Have you ever, ever, ever,

in your long-legged life

met a long-legged sailor

with a long-legged wife?

No, I never, never, never,

in my long-legged life

met a long-legged sailor

with a long-legged wife.

Have you ever, ever, ever,

in your short-legged life...

Have you ever, ever, ever,

knock-kneed life...

Have you ever, ever, ever,

pigeon-toed life...

Have you ever, ever, ever,

bow-legged life...

Hush, Little Baby

Hush, little baby, don't say a word,
Papa's gonna buy you a mockingbird.

If that mockingbird don't sing,
Papa's gonna buy you a diamond ring.

If that diamond ring turns brass,
Papa's gonna buy you a looking-glass.

If that looking-glass gets broke,
Papa's gonna buy you a billy goat.

If that billy goat don't pull,

Papa's gonna buy you a cart and mule.

If that cart and mule turn over,

Papa's gonna buy you a dog named Rover.

If that dog named Rover won't bark,

Papa's gonna buy you a horse and cart.

If that horse and cart fall down,

You'll still be the sweetest little baby
in town.

Rock-a-Bye, Baby

Rock-a-bye, baby, on the treetop,

When the wind blows, the cradle will rock;

When the bough breaks, the cradle will fall;

Down will come baby, cradle and all.

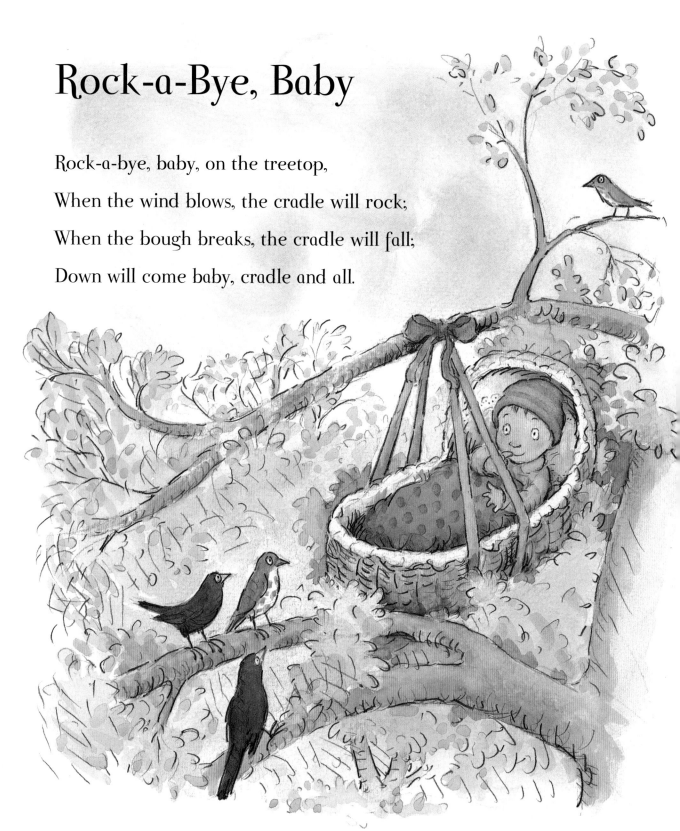

Little Fred

When little Fred went to bed,

He always said his prayers;

He kissed Mama, then Papa,

And straightaway went upstairs.

Miss Mary Mack

Miss Mary Mack,

All dressed in black,

With silver buttons

All down her back,

She asked her mother

For fifty pence,

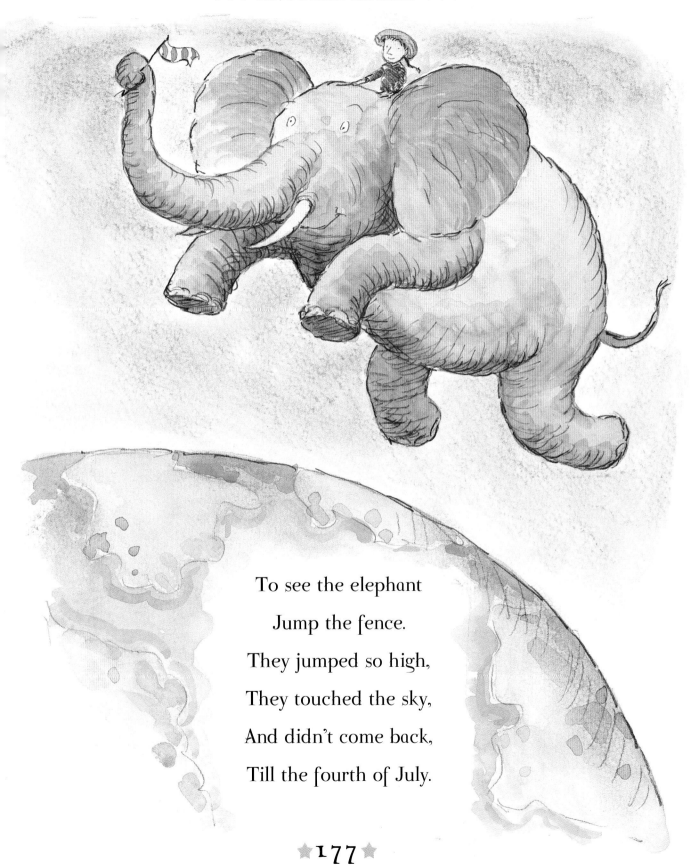

To see the elephant
Jump the fence.
They jumped so high,
They touched the sky,
And didn't come back,
Till the fourth of July.

Bed in Summer

In winter I get up at night
And dress by yellow candlelight.
In summer, quite the other way,
I have to go to bed by day.

I have to go to bed and see
The birds still hopping on the tree,
Or hear the grown-up people's feet
Still going past me in the street.

And does it not seem hard to you,

When all the sky is clear and blue,

And I should like so much to play,

To have to go to bed by day?

—Robert Louis Stevenson

Ten in the Bed

There were ten in the bed and the little one said,

"Roll over, roll over."

So they all rolled over and one fell out.

There were nine in the bed and the little one said,

"Roll over, roll over."

So they all rolled over and one fell out.

There were eight in the bed and the little one said,

"Roll over, roll over."

So they all rolled over and one fell out.

There were seven in the bed and the little one said,

"Roll over, roll over."

So they all rolled over and one fell out.

There were six in the bed and the little one said,

"Roll over, roll over."

So they all rolled over and one fell out.

There were five in the bed and the little one said,

"Roll over, roll over."

So they all rolled over and one fell out.

There were four in the bed and the little one said,

"Roll over, roll over."

So they all rolled over and one fell out.

There were three in the bed and the little one said,

"Roll over, roll over."

So they all rolled over and one fell out.

There were two in the bed and the little one said,

"Roll over, roll over."

So they all rolled over and one fell out.

There was one in the bed and the little one said,

"Good night!"

There Was a Crooked Man

There was a crooked man,
and he walked a crooked mile.

He found a crooked sixpence
upon a crooked stile.

He bought a crooked cat,
which caught a crooked mouse,

And they all lived together
in a little crooked house.

Sleep Little Child

Sleep little child, go to sleep,

Mother is here by your bed.

Sleep little child, go to sleep,

Rest on the pillow your head.

The world is silent and still,

The moon shines bright on the hill,

Then creeps past the windowsill.

Sleep little child, go to sleep,

Oh sleep, go to sleep.

Tweedledum and Tweedledee

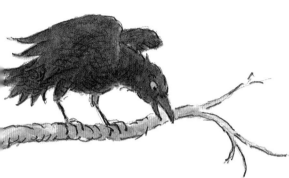

Tweedledum and Tweedledee

Agreed to have a battle;

For Tweedledum said Tweedledee

Had spoiled his nice new rattle.

Just then flew down a monstrous crow,

As black as a tar-barrel;

Which frightened both the heroes so,

They quite forgot their quarrel.

Three Young Rats

Three young rats with black felt hats,

Three young ducks with white straw flats,

Three young dogs with curling tails,

Three young cats with demi-veils,

Went out to walk with two young pigs

In satin vests and sorrel wigs,

But suddenly it chanced to rain

And so they all went home again.

Star Light, Star Bright

Star light, star bright,

First star I see tonight,

I wish I may, I wish I might,

Have the wish I wish tonight.

Index of First Lines